MARVEL

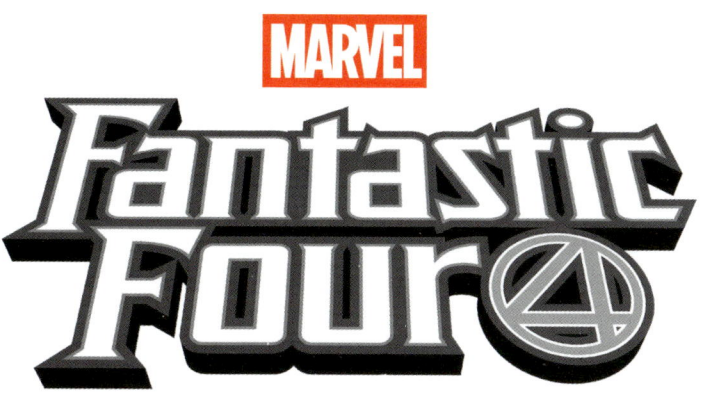

Fantastic Four

Cosmic Adventures

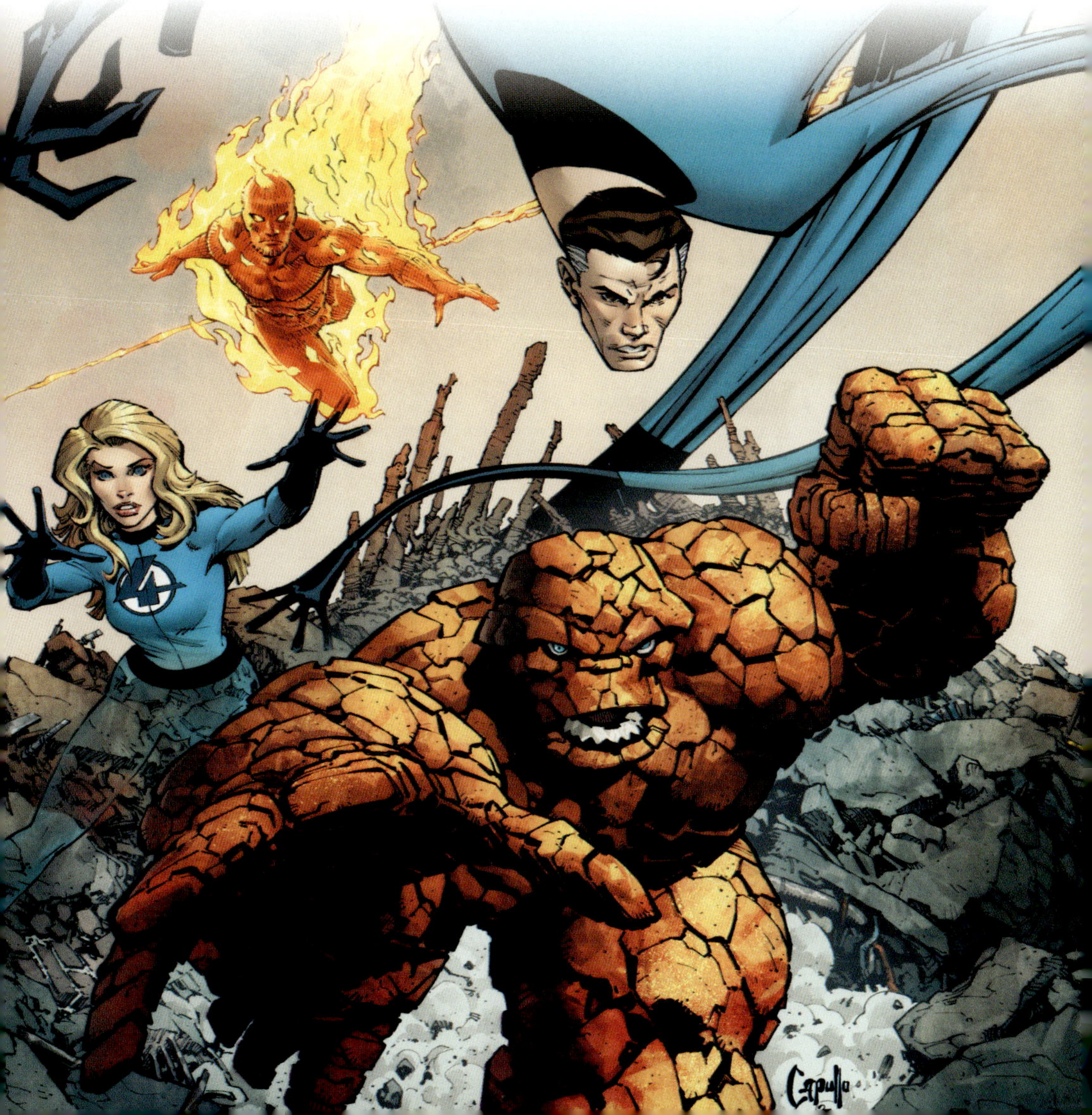

Senior Editor Ruth Amos
Project Art Editor Jon Hall
Proofreader Lori Hand
Production Editor Siu Yin Chan
Senior Production Controller Laura Andrews
Managing Editor Emma Grange
Managing Art Editor Vicky Short
Publisher Paula Regan
Art Director Charlotte Coulais
Managing Director Mark Searle

Designed for DK by Gary Gilbert
Reading consultant Barbara Marinak

First American Edition, 2025
Published in the United States by DK Publishing,
a division of Penguin Random House LLC
1745 Broadway, 20th Floor, New York, NY 10019

Page design copyright © 2025 Dorling Kindersley Limited
25 26 27 28 29 10 9 8 7 6 5 4 3 2 1
001–345013–July/2025

© 2025 MARVEL

Without limiting the rights under the copyright reserved above, no part of this publication may be reproduced, stored in or introduced into a retrieval system, or transmitted, in any form, or by any means (electronic, mechanical, photocopying, recording, or otherwise), without the prior written permission of the copyright owner. Published in Great Britain by Dorling Kindersley Limited

ISBN 978-0-5939-6081-3 (paperback)
ISBN 978-0-5939-6082-0 (hardcover)

DK books are available at special discounts when purchased in bulk for sales promotions, premiums, fund-raising, or educational use. For details, contact: DK Publishing Special Markets, 1745 Broadway, 20th Floor, New York, NY 10019
SpecialSales@dk.com

Printed and bound in China

www.dk.com
www.marvel.com

This book was made with Forest Stewardship Council™ certified paper—one small step in DK's commitment to a sustainable future.
Learn more at www.dk.com/uk/information/sustainability

MARVEL
Fantastic Four
Cosmic Adventures

Written by Melanie Scott

Contents

6	Meet the Fantastic Four
8	Fantastic Four origins
10	Space and time
12	Mister Fantastic
14	The Invisible Woman
16	The Human Torch
18	The Thing
20	High-tech heroes

22	Fantastic family
24	Special uniforms
26	Best friends
28	Heroes in the city
30	Substitutes
32	The Maker
34	The Future Foundation
36	Team-ups
38	Doctor Doom
40	Mole Man
42	Galactus and Silver Surfer
44	Heroes and explorers
46	Glossary
47	Index
48	Quiz

Meet the Fantastic Four

Mister Fantastic, the Invisible Woman, the Human Torch, and the Thing are the Fantastic Four team! They are brave, loyal, and tough.

Mister Fantastic

The Human Torch

However, their greatest powers might be their close family bond and their love for each other.

The Thing

The Invisible Woman

Fantastic Four origins

The Fantastic Four get their super-powers from cosmic rays. One day, they went on a mission in a spaceship. The rays hit their spaceship as it left Earth's atmosphere. After they crash-landed, they realized they had gained amazing abilities! They promised to use their powers to help people as a team.

Super Hero promise

Space and time

The Fantastic Four go on adventures across the universe. They even travel to alternate universes! They always try to make friends with the people they meet. The team uses their trips to discover more about science. They have also traveled in time.

Space voyage

Mister Fantastic

Reed Richards is the leader of the Fantastic Four. His code name is Mister Fantastic. He can stretch his body into all shapes and sizes, like elastic.

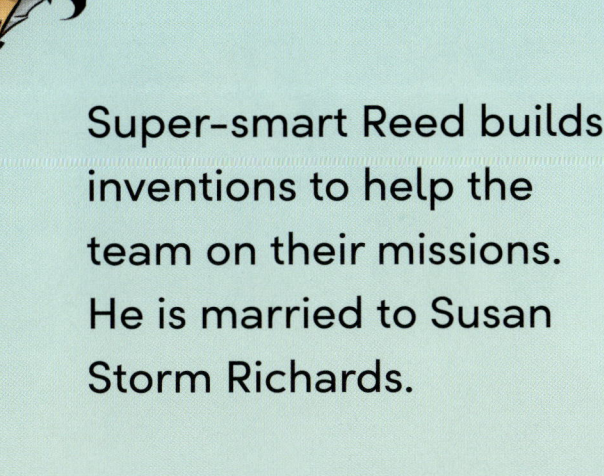

Super-smart Reed builds inventions to help the team on their missions. He is married to Susan Storm Richards.

The Invisible Woman

Susan Storm Richards, also known as the Invisible Woman, can do a lot more than turn invisible! Sue uses force fields to protect herself and her teammates. She also creates platforms of energy to lift herself and others high into the air.

Force fields

The Human Torch

The Human Torch, also known as Johnny Storm, has incredible flame powers. He can make shapes from fire and is able to fly. Johnny is Susan's brother. He loves cars and playing pranks on his teammate, the Thing. However, he also knows when it is time to get serious for a mission.

The Thing

Ben Grimm is the Thing—a brave hero! He has rocky skin and is very good at flying airplanes and spaceships. He loves being strong enough to protect his friends. Ben is married to Alicia Masters and they have adopted two children.

Expert pilot

High-tech heroes

The Fantastic Four use great gadgets and amazing vehicles.

Fantasti-Car
There have been several different Fantasti-Cars. The Human Torch loves to fix them and make them even better.

The Lab
Every Fantastic Four base has a laboratory. Here, Mister Fantastic studies science and works on inventions. The Thing can lift any heavy parts for him!

H.E.R.B.I.E.
(Highly Engineered Robot Built for Interdimensional Exploration)
The team's robot companion uses advanced alien technology. He can also fly and connect with any computer system.

Baxter Building
The team's main headquarters is in a tower in New York City. It is packed with highly advanced technology to protect and help them.

Fantastic family

The Fantastic Four are all about family! As well as the four heroes, their family includes the Skrull N'Kalla and the Kree Jo-Venn. They are the children of Ben and his wife, Alicia.

Other members include Reed and Sue's children—Franklin and Valeria.

Special uniforms

The team's uniforms are made from unstable molecules. They are specially designed to adapt to each member's powers.

Fireproof material

Super-stretchy fabric

The uniforms also contain universal translators. These allow the team to understand any language, whether on Earth or other planets.

Team symbol

Material can turn invisible

Best friends

Outside of the Fantastic Four, the Human Torch's best friend is Spider-Man (Peter Parker). The two young heroes like to hang out together in New York City. The pair swaps stories of their adventures. They were even roommates for a while!

Spider-Mobile
The Human Torch loves cars, so he builds Spider-Man a customized vehicle. He has to teach his buddy how to drive.

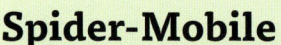

Heroes in the city

New York City is the hometown of the Fantastic Four. They do not have secret identities, so New Yorkers often see them around the city. The team has had bases on Pier Four by the Hudson River, in the Yancy Street neighborhood, in the Baxter Building, and in the Four Freedoms Plaza.

Hometown
The Thing grew up in the Yancy Street neighborhood. He has a bad habit of causing chaos when he's back there.

Substitutes

Sometimes the members of the Fantastic Four must leave the team for a while. Luckily, their heroic friends can step in to help.

Ant-Man
When the original group goes on a long mission away from Earth, Ant-Man (Scott Lang) leads an all-new team until they return.

She-Hulk
The Fantastic Four's lawyer, She-Hulk (Jennifer Walters), replaced the Thing for a long time while he was away in space.

Black Panther
Black Panther (T'Challa) is the king of Wakanda. He is a friend and ally of the team. He also joined the group for a short time when Reed was away.

Spider-Man
Spider-Man is one of the group's most trusted allies. He volunteers to help the team when they need him.

The Maker

In an alternate universe, there is a version of Mister Fantastic who turned evil. He is called the Maker. He comes to the Fantastic Four's Earth to cause trouble.

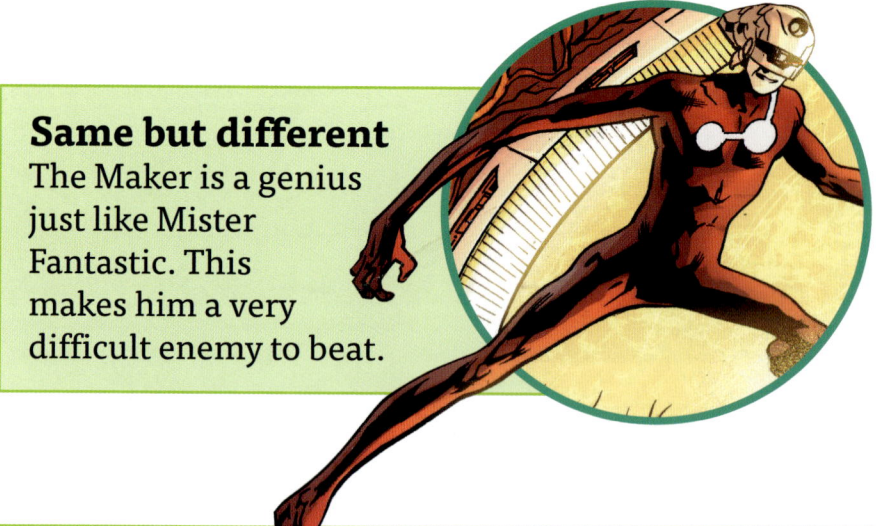

Same but different
The Maker is a genius just like Mister Fantastic. This makes him a very difficult enemy to beat.

The Future Foundation

Mister Fantastic sets up a school for young super-powered beings. They learn how to be the best heroes they can be!

The school is called the Future Foundation. It is based in the Fantastic Four's headquarters in New York City.

Team-ups

Sometimes the Fantastic Four team up with other heroes like the Avengers for important missions. Mister Fantastic is also part of a secret club called the Illuminati. They use their intelligence and powers to protect Earth from danger.

Spy duo
The Invisible Woman has worked as a spy with the Super Hero Black Widow.

Doctor Doom

Doctor Doom is the ruler of the country Latveria. He is very smart and can cast powerful magic spells. Although he is the Fantastic Four's enemy, he is also Valeria Richards' godfather!

Godfather Doom
Doctor Doom helps at the birth of the Invisible Woman and Mister Fantastic's daughter. They let him choose her name, Valeria.

Mole Man

The Mole Man rules the underground kingdom of Subterranea. He lives in caves and tunnels and can command scary monsters. He tries to invade the surface world, but the Fantastic Four stop him on their very first mission.

Mole Man's monsters

Galactus and Silver Surfer

Galactus is one of the Fantastic Four's most powerful enemies. He is also known as the World-Eater, because he is so big that he eats planets! The Fantastic Four have saved Earth from his hunger several times.

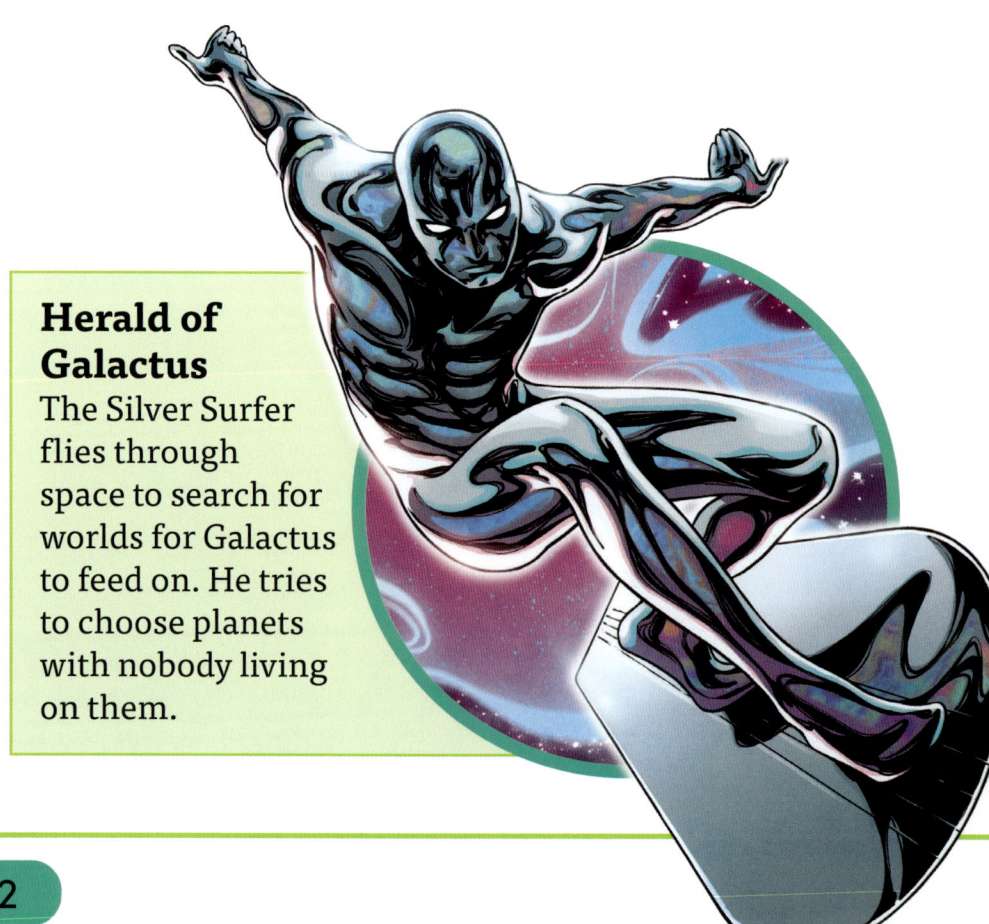

Herald of Galactus
The Silver Surfer flies through space to search for worlds for Galactus to feed on. He tries to choose planets with nobody living on them.

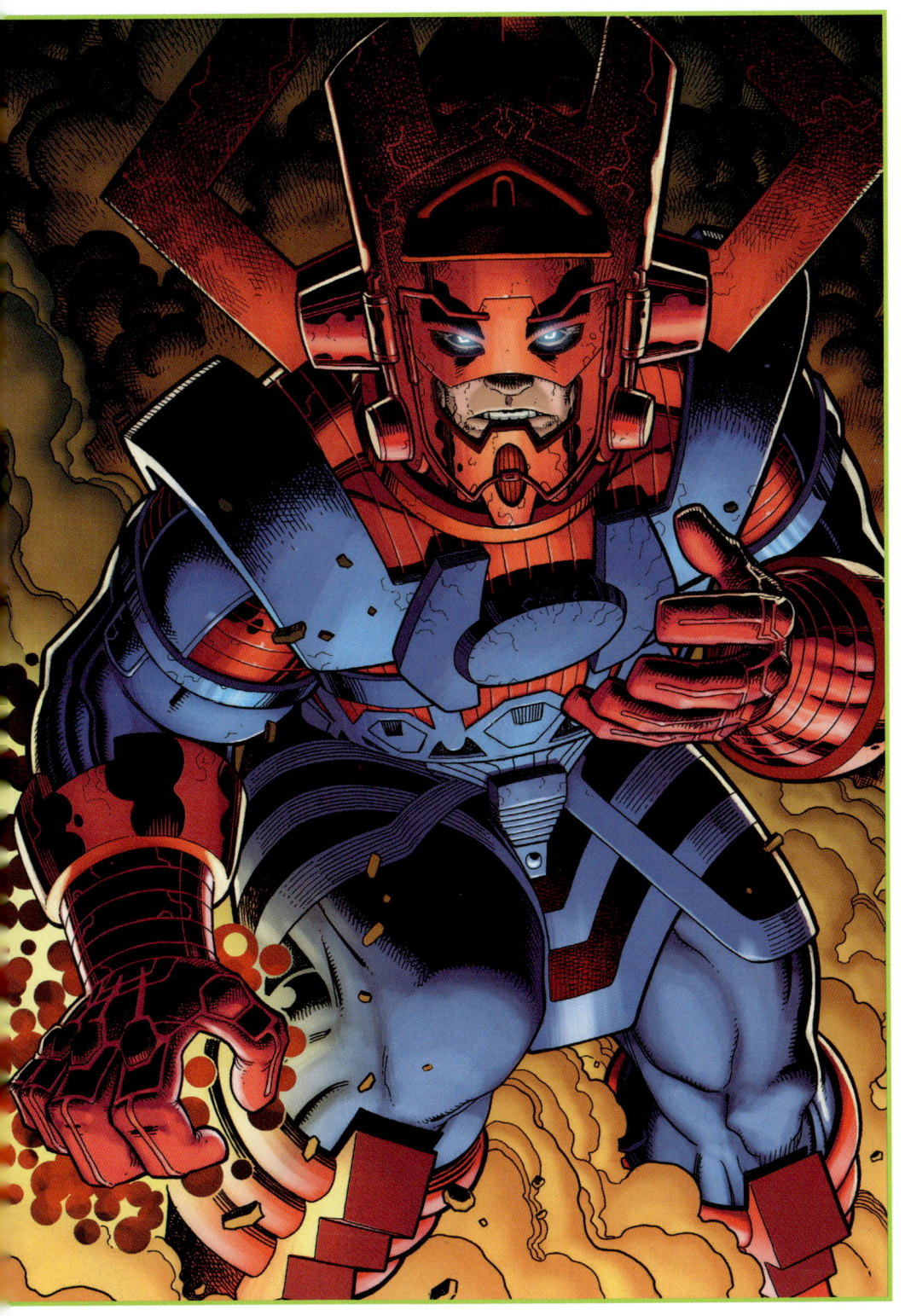

Heroes and explorers

The Fantastic Four is a team like no other! They love to explore new worlds and even new dimensions to find out more about the universe. These Super Heroes have vowed to use their powers to protect people from evil. But most important of all, they are a family.

Glossary

atmosphere
a layer of gases that surrounds the Earth

cosmic
of or relating to the universe

cosmic rays
particles that speed through outer space

customized
changed to suit a person's needs

dimension
a different reality in space and time

headquarters
the main base of a team or organization

interdimensional
between dimensions

invention
a new machine or process that hasn't been created before

laboratory
a room containing scientific equipment

lawyer
a person whose job is to help people understand the law

mission
a special task that someone is sent somewhere to do

molecule
a small particle, made of two or more atoms joined together

technology
machines that help make life better

unstable
something that is not fixed or steady and is likely to change

volunteers
offers to help

vowed
made a promise to do something

Index

Alicia Masters 19, 22

Ant-Man 30

Avengers 37

Baxter Building 21, 29

Black Panther 31

Black Widow 37

cosmic rays 8

Doctor Doom 38-39

Fantasti-Car 20

Franklin 23

Future Foundation 34-35

Galactus 42-43

H.E.R.B.I.E. 21

the Human Torch 6-7, 16-17, 20, 26-27

Illuminati 37

the Invisible Woman 6-7, 14-15, 37, 38

Jo-Venn 22

laboratory 20

Latveria 38

the Maker 32-33

Mister Fantastic 6-7, 12-13, 20, 32, 34, 37, 38

Mole Man 40-41

New York City 21, 26, 28-29, 35

N'Kalla 22

She-Hulk 30

Silver Surfer 42

Spider-Man (Peter Parker) 26-27, 31

Spider-Mobile 26

Subterranea 40

the Thing 6-7, 16, 18-19, 20, 29, 30

uniforms 24-25

Valeria 23, 38

Yancy Street 29

Quiz

Are you a Fantastic Four expert? Try the quiz to find out!

1. Which Fantastic Four member can create force fields?
2. What are the Fantastic Four's uniforms made from?
3. Who is the Human Torch's best friend?
4. Which city do the Fantastic Four live in?
5. Who is Valeria Richards' godfather?

1. The Invisible Woman 2. Unstable molecules 3. Spider-Man (Peter Parker) 4. New York City 5. Doctor Doom